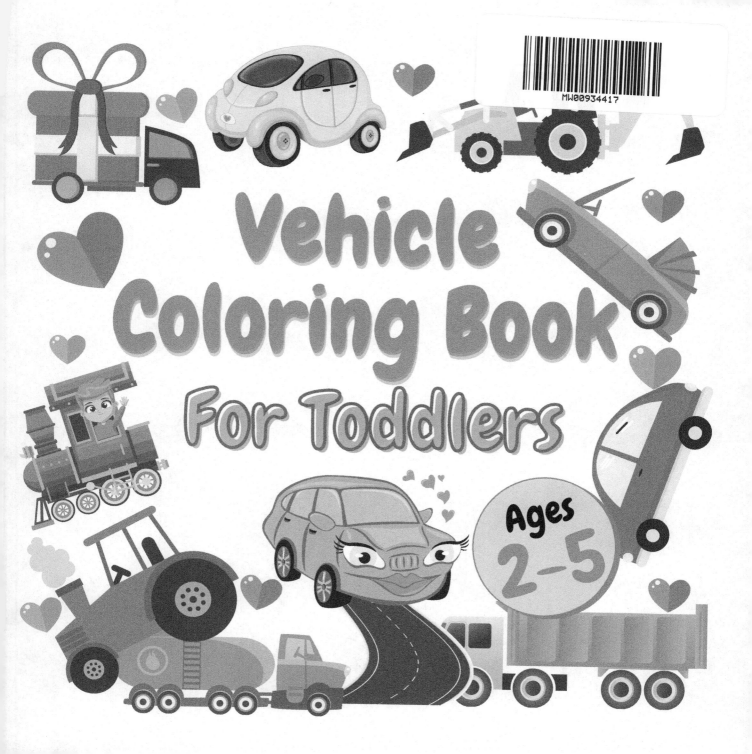

Vehicle Coloring Book
For Toddlers

Ages 2-5

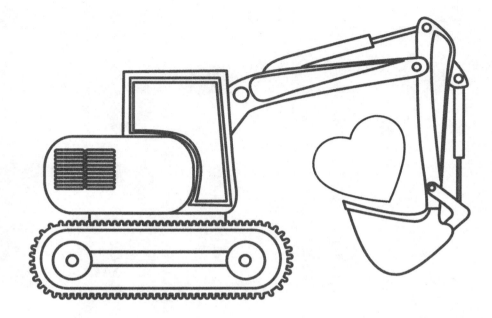

THIS BOOK
BELONGS TO:

ooooooooooooooooooooooooooooooooooooooo

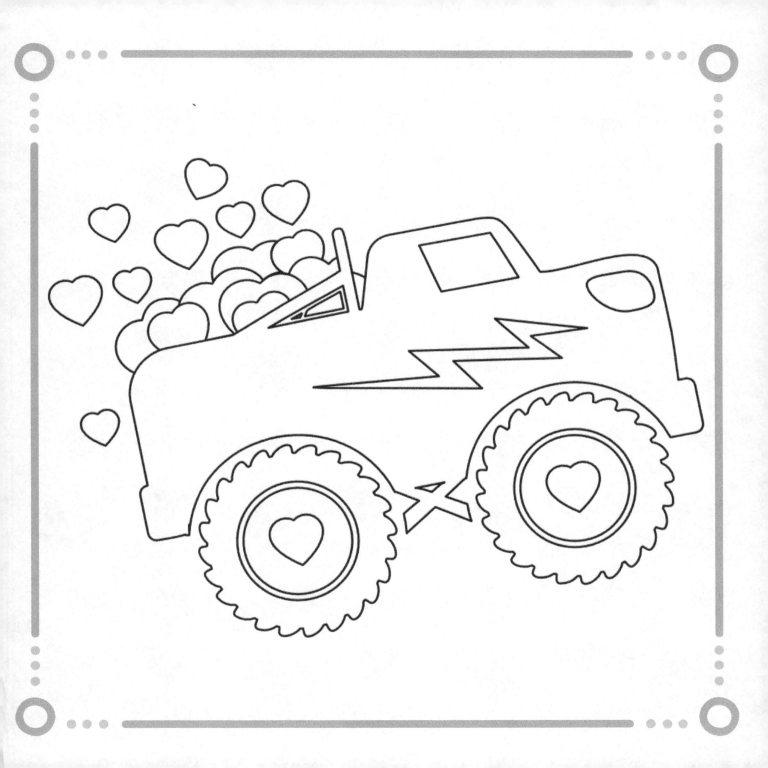

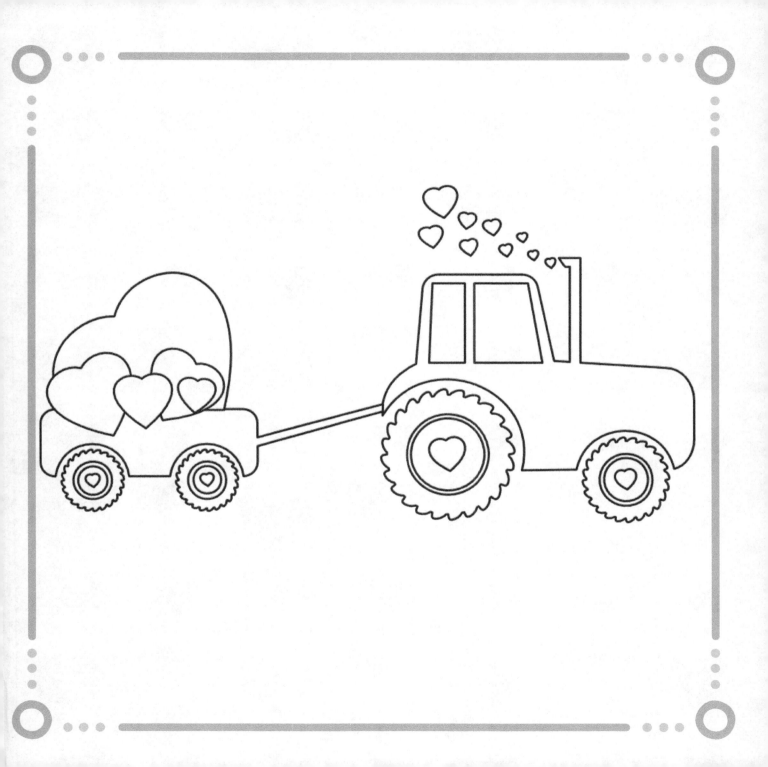

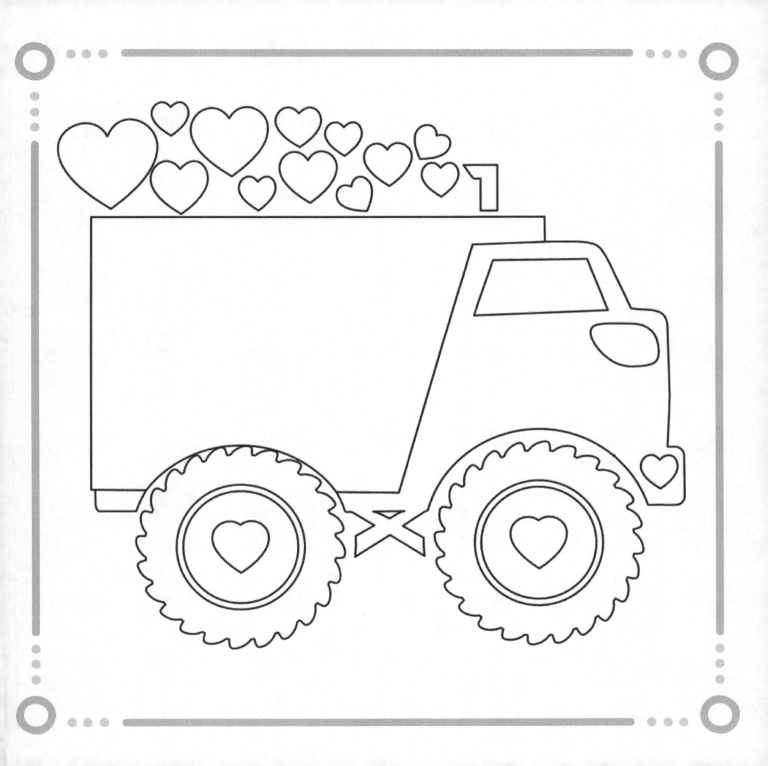

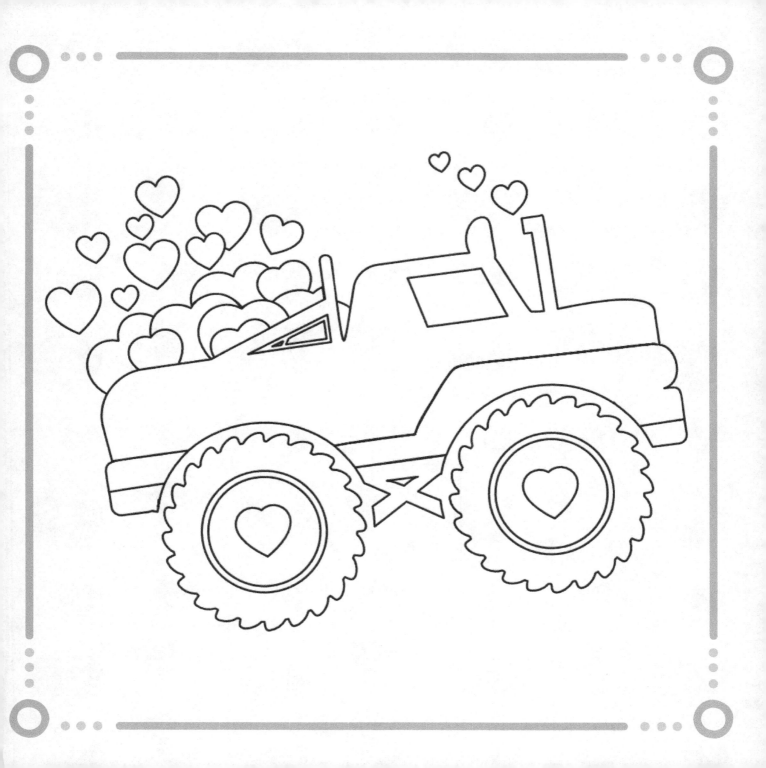

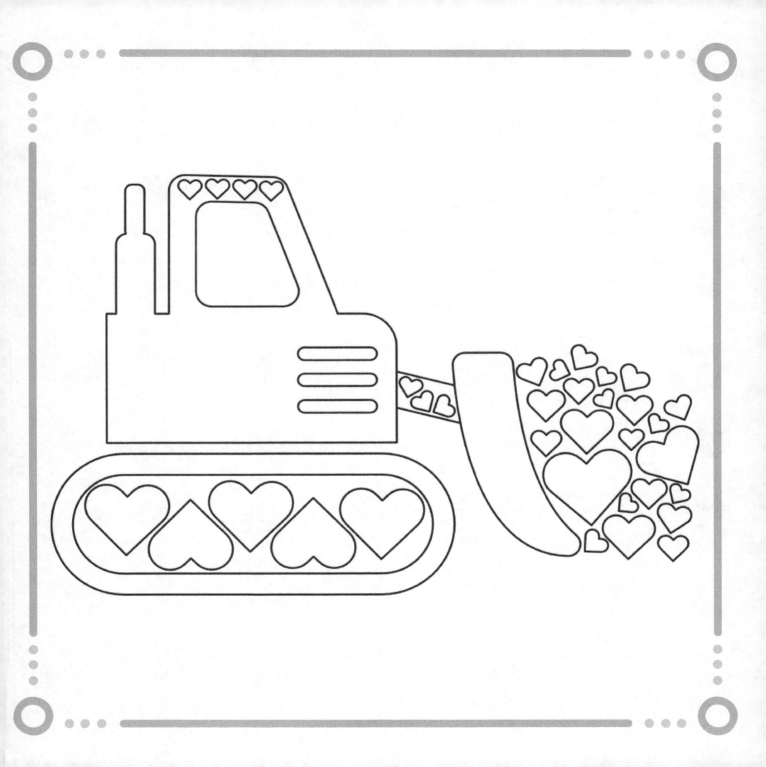

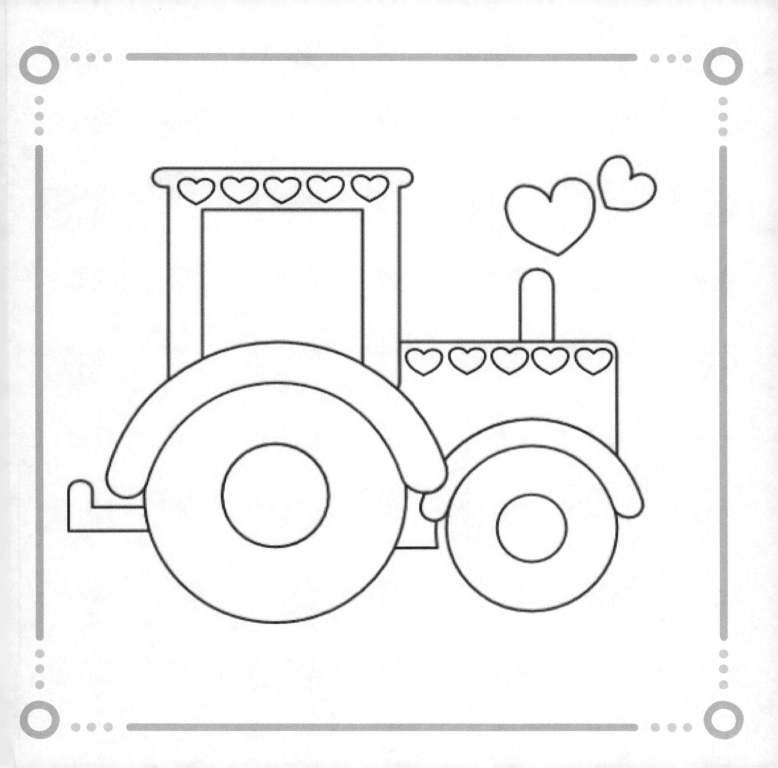

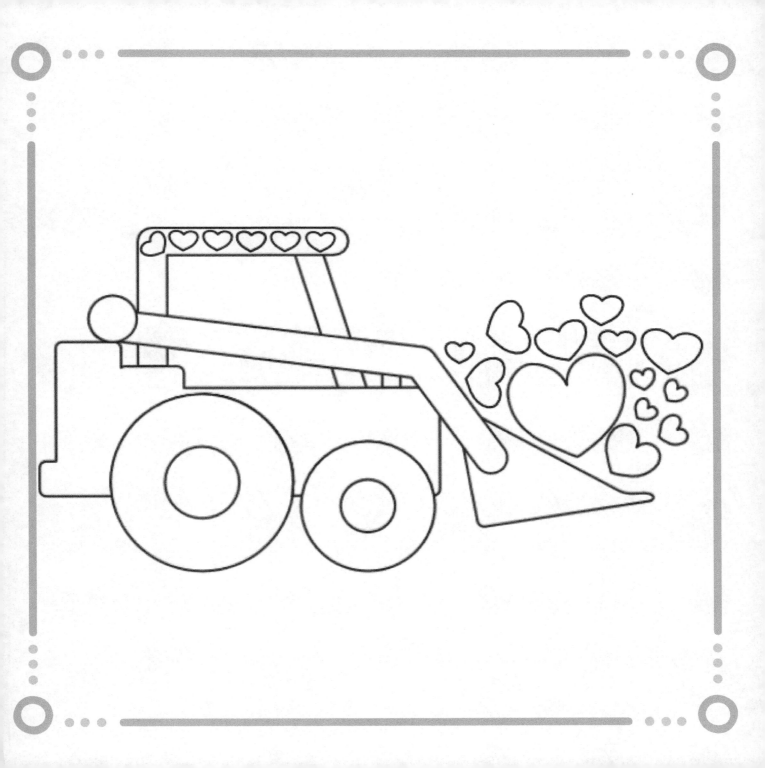

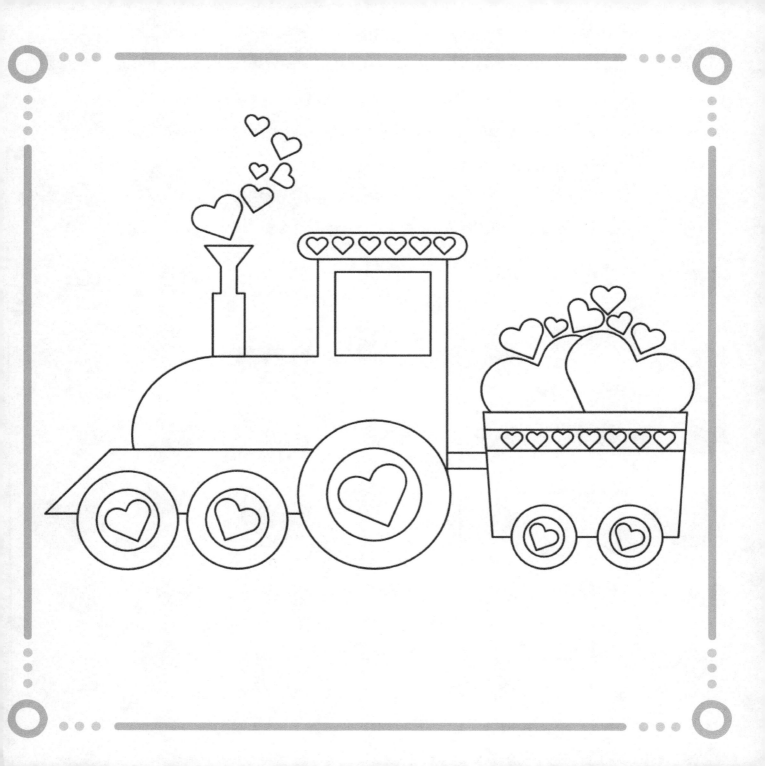

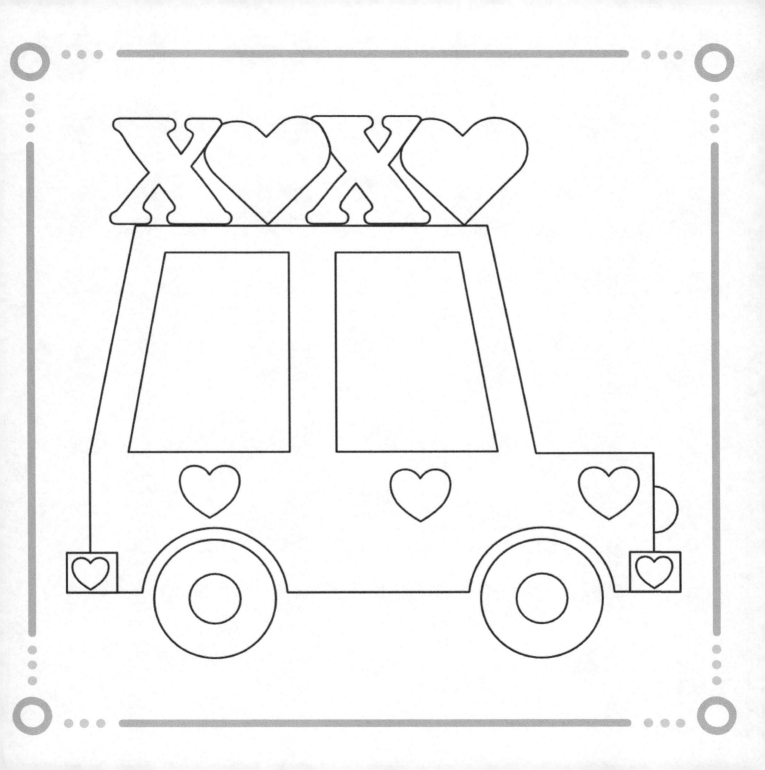

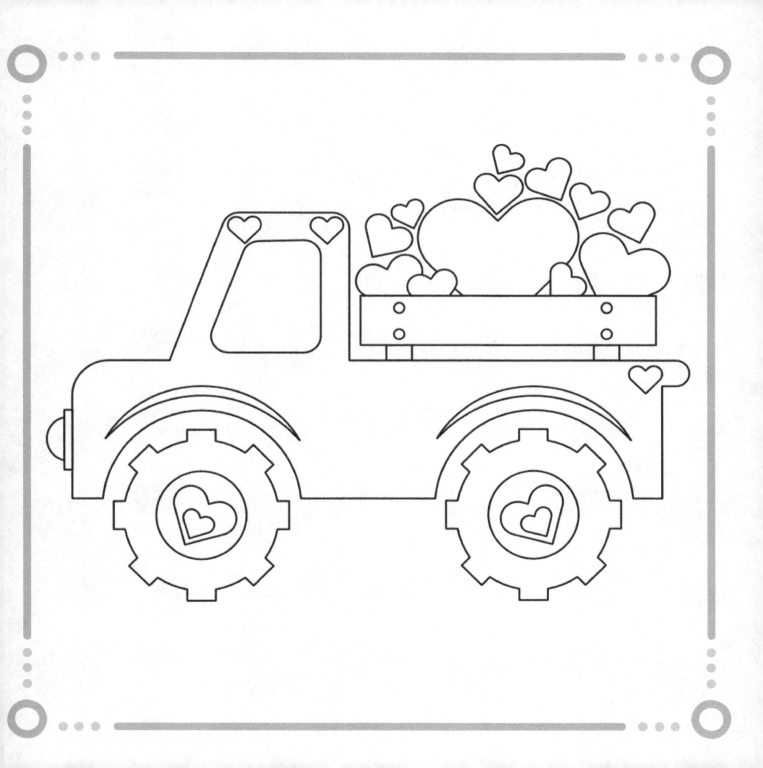

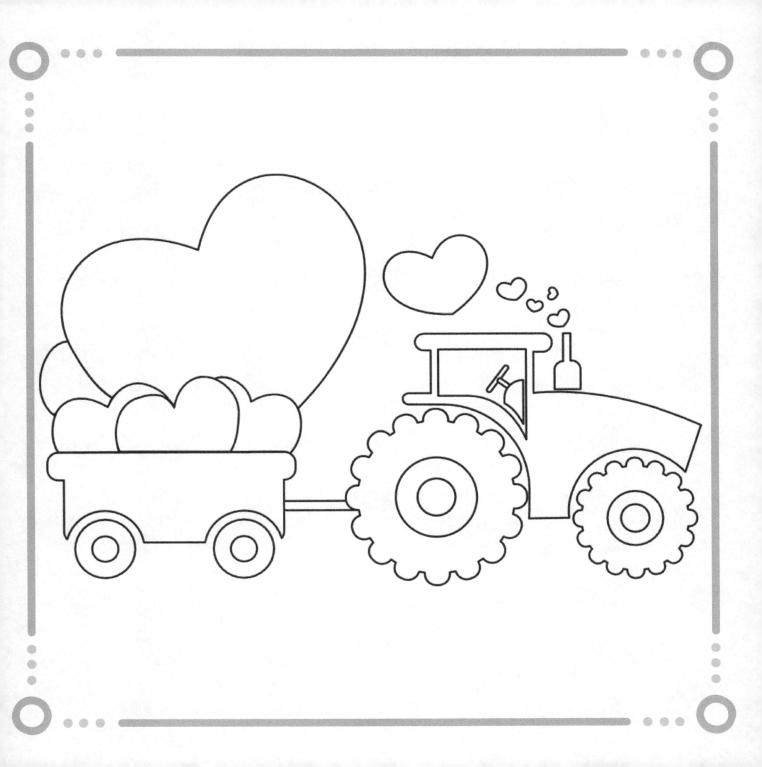

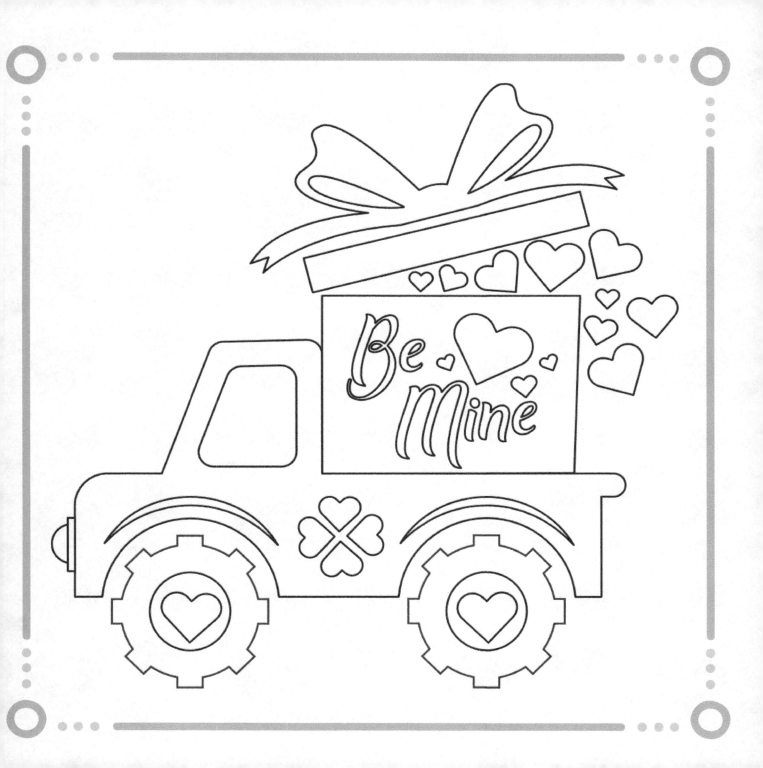

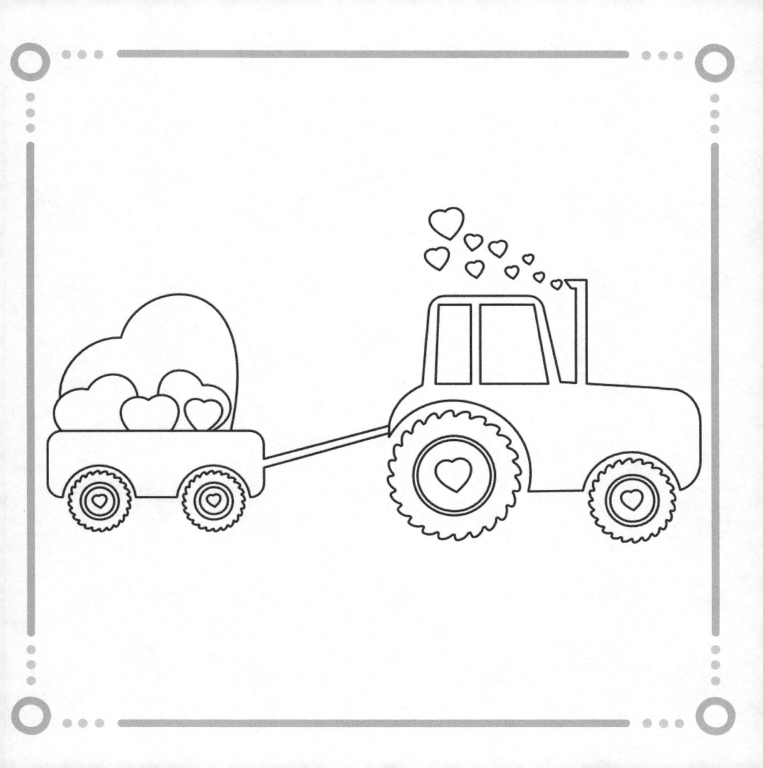

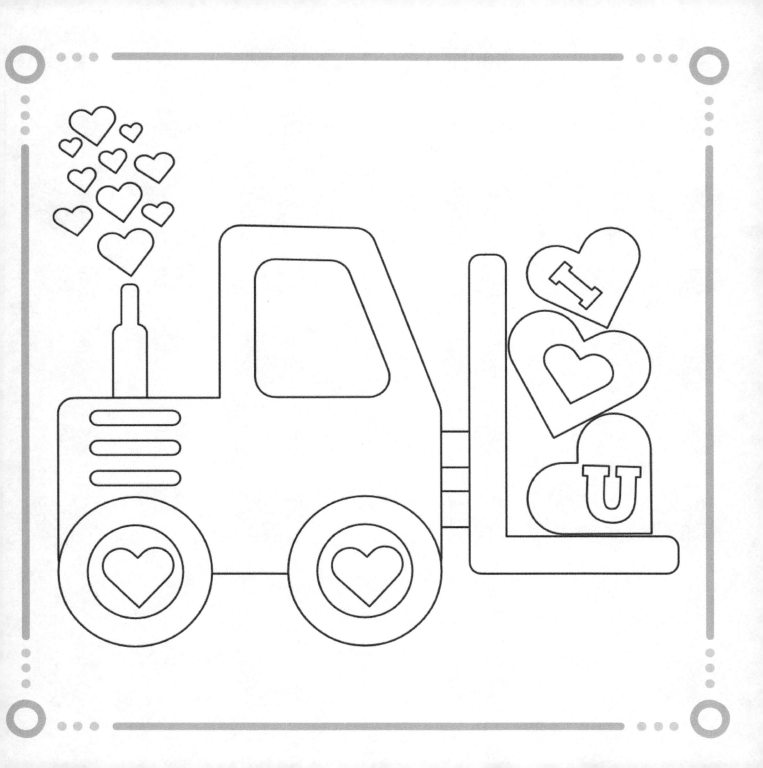

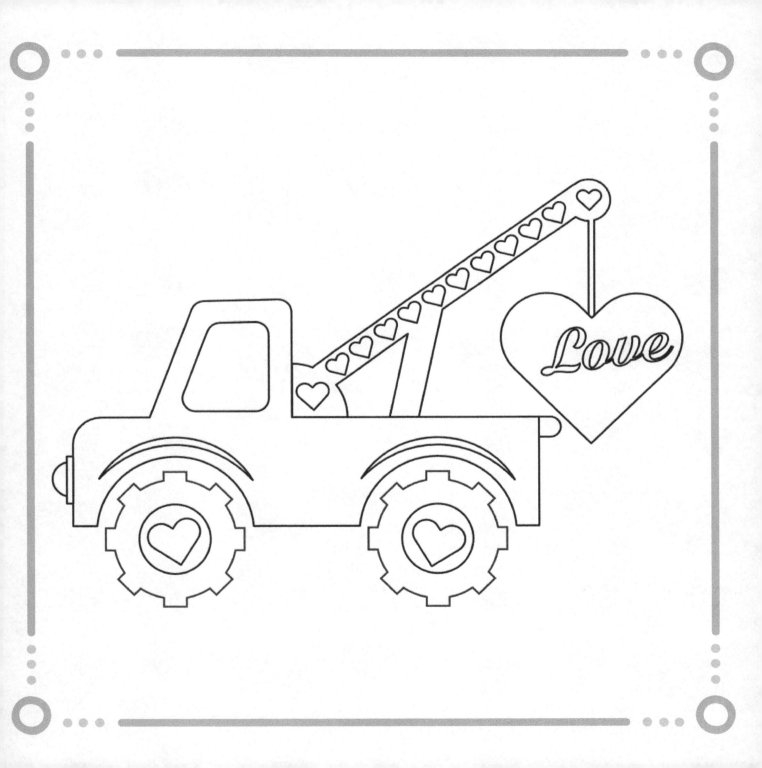

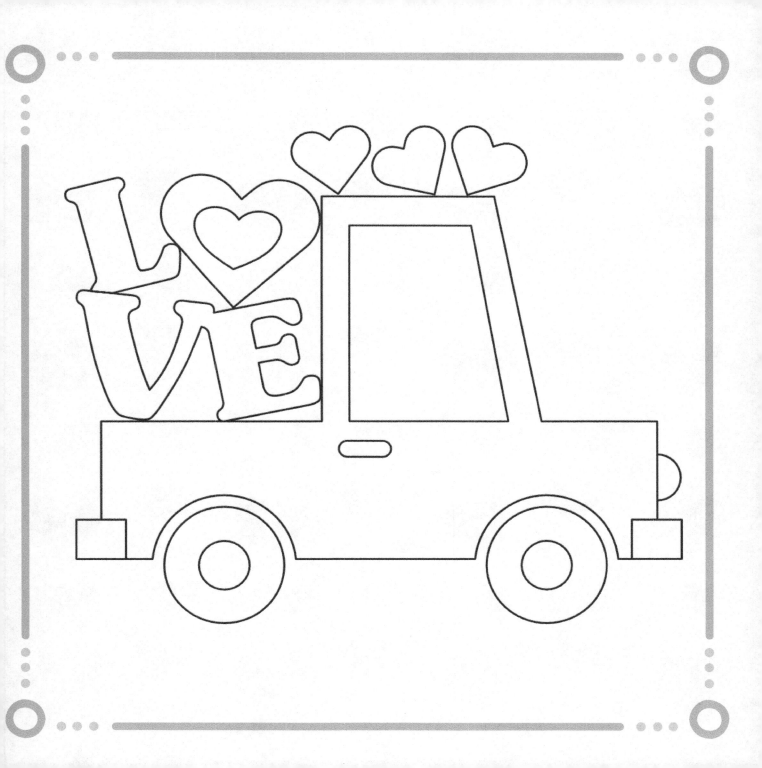

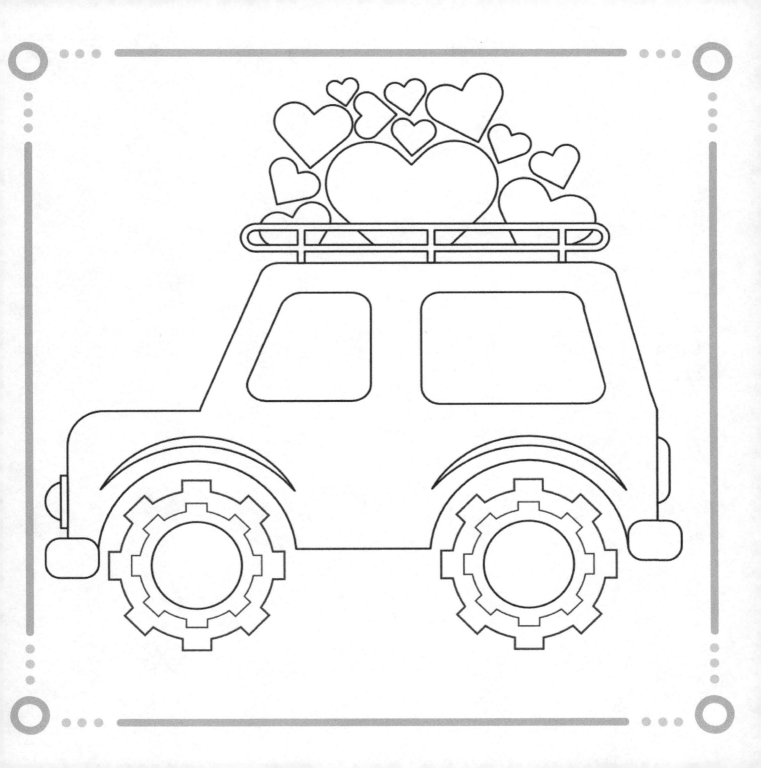

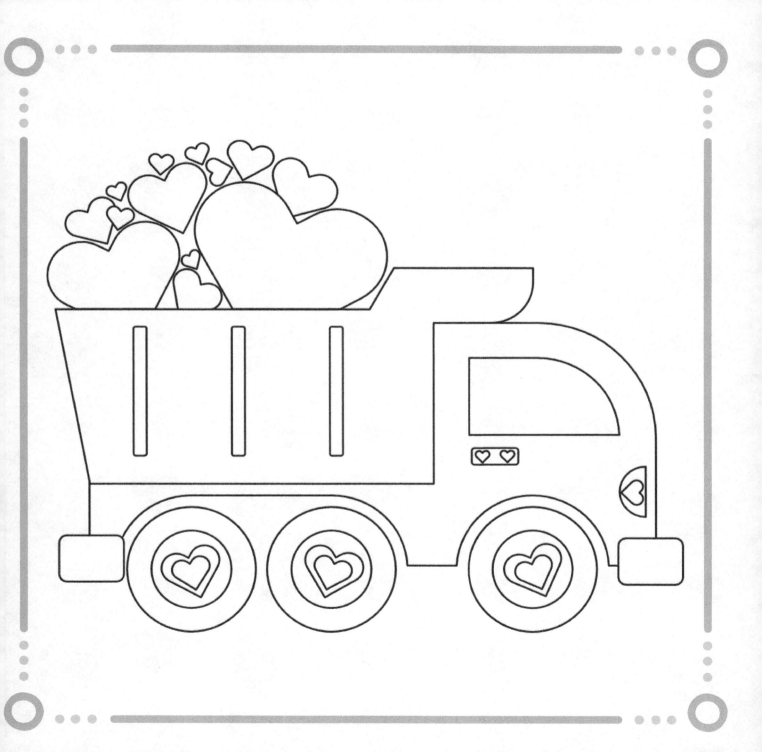

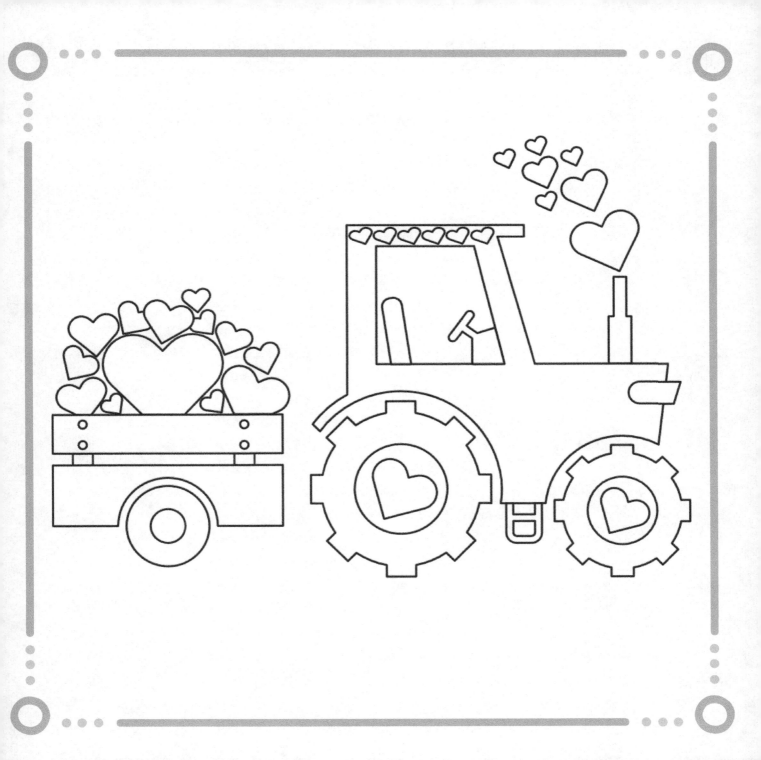

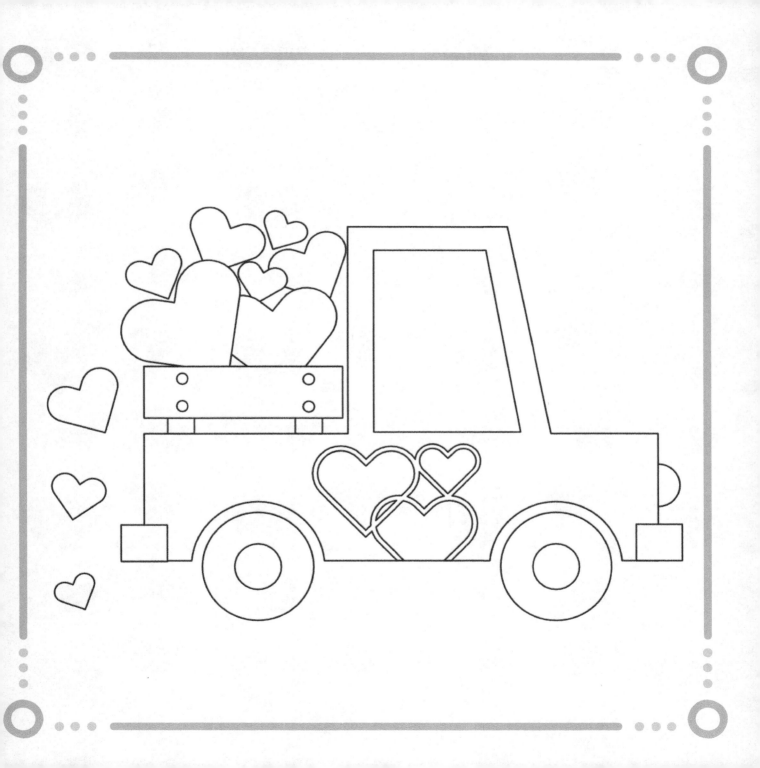

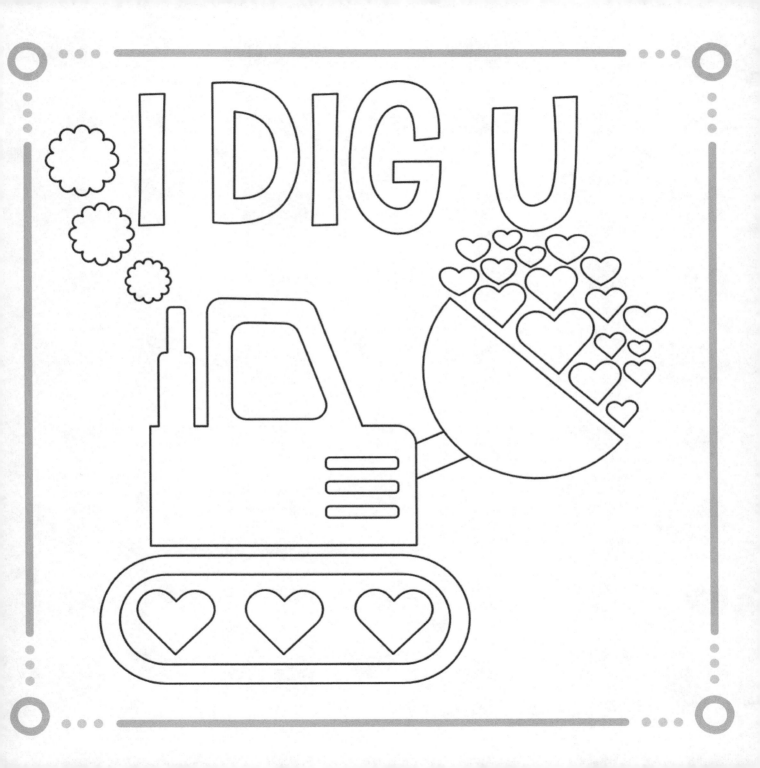

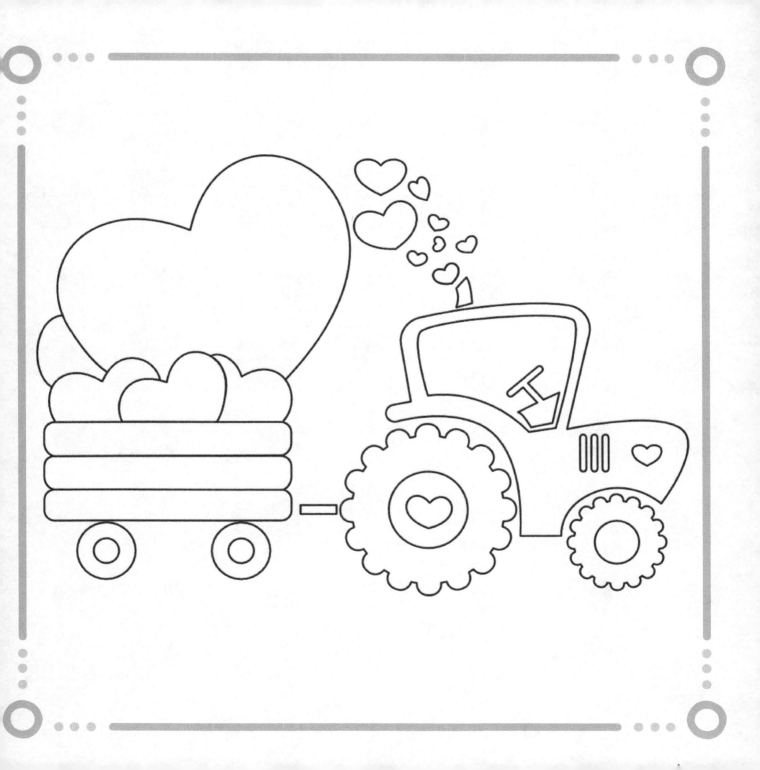

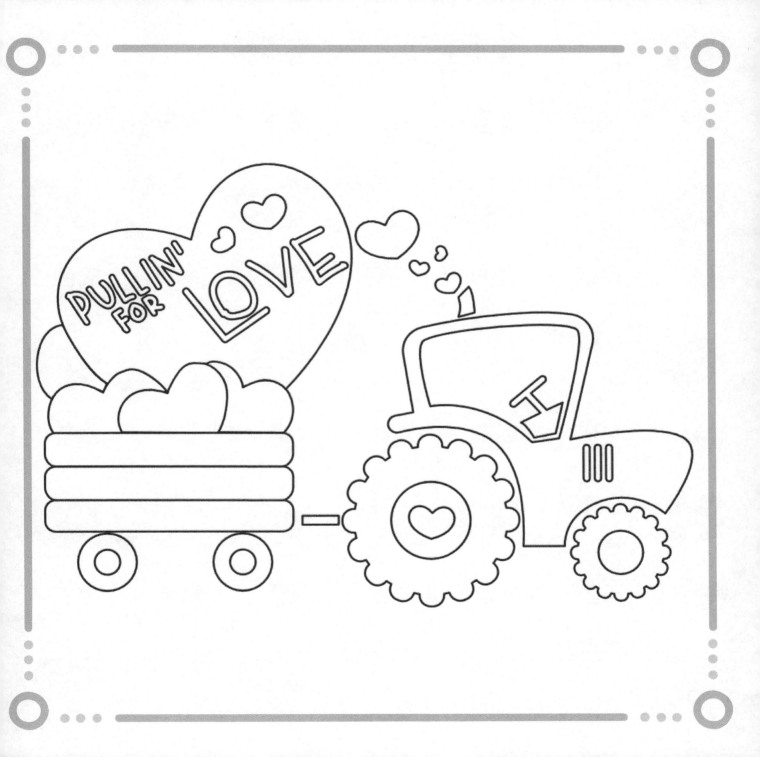

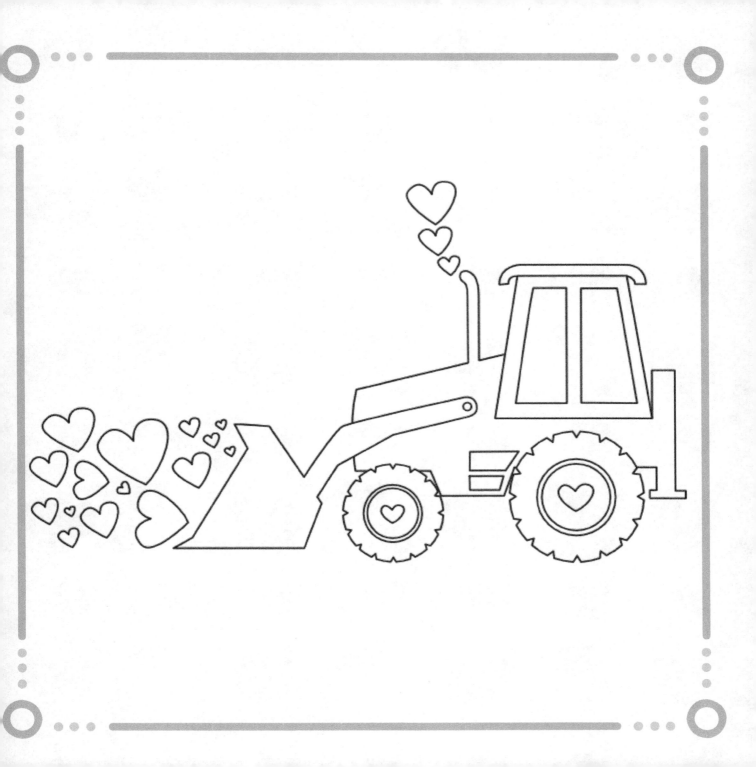

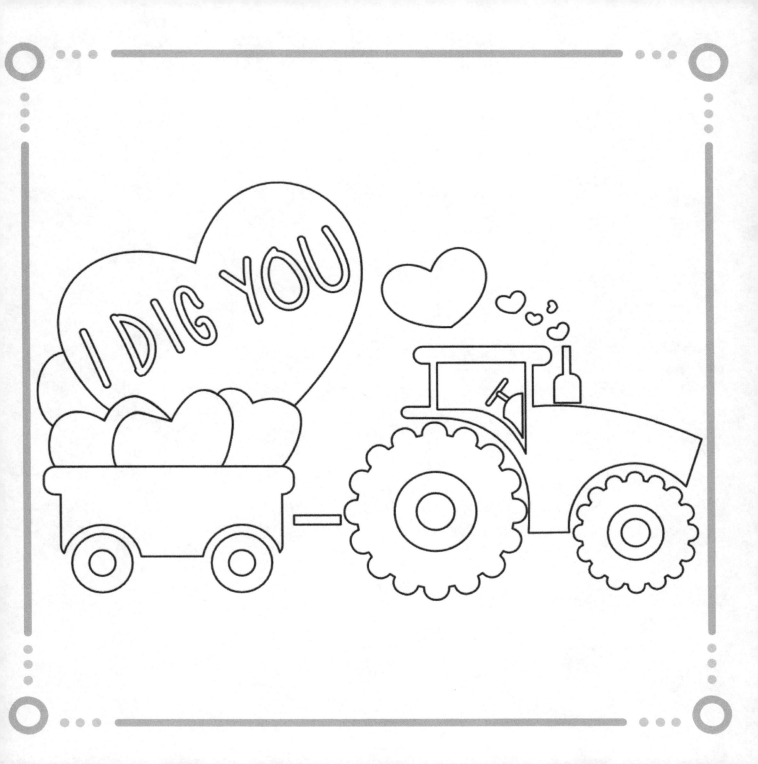

Happy Valentine's Day !

Please leave a review -
I'd love to know it!

Made in the USA
Coppell, TX
05 February 2024